T0368479

DRAGON SLAYING

for Kids

GRACE M. M. JAEGER

WestBow Press books may be ordered through booksellers or by contacting:

WestBow Press
A Division of Thomas Nelson & Zondervan
1663 Liberty Drive
Bloomington, IN 47403
www.westbowpress.com
1 (866) 928-1240

ISBN: 978-1-5127-2139-3 (sc)
ISBN: 978-1-5127-2140-9 (e)

Library of Congress Control Number: 2015919572

Print information available on the last page.

WestBow Press rev. date: 12/14/2015

WESTBOW
PRESS®
A DIVISION OF THOMAS NELSON
& ZONDERVAN

This book is dedicated to my brothers, Bo, Dakota, Jericho, Everett, Oakley, and my sister Laine; as well as the Goodwyn boys, and all the children that dared to like dragons and follow God's will.

CONTENTS

Fear ~ 2

Selfishness ~ 6

Bitterness ~ 10

Laziness ~ 14

Pride ~ 18

Idolatry ~ 22

Deceitfulness ~ 26

Disobedience ~ 30

Worry ~ 34

Greed ~ 38

Dishonor ~ 42

Indiscipline ~ 46

Unkindness ~ 50

'Stand up, stand up for Jesus; stand in His strength alone

The arm of flesh will fail you; you dare not trust your own

Put on the gospel armor; each piece put on with prayer

When duty calls or danger, be never wanting there.'

Stand up, Stand up For Jesus, verse 3, words by George Duffield Jr.

'For the Word of God is living and active and sharper than any two-edged sword, and piercing as far as the division of soul and spirit, of both joints and marrow, and able to judge the thoughts and intentions of the heart.'

Hebrews 4:12

"Behold, I have given you authority to tread on serpents and scorpions, and over all the power of the enemy, and nothing will injure you."

Luke 10:19

'Finally, my brethren, be strong in the Lord and in the power of His might. Put on the whole armor of God, that you may be able to stand against the wiles of the devil. For we do not wrestle against flesh and blood, but against principalities, against powers, against the rulers of the darkness of this age, against spiritual hosts of wickedness in the heavenly places. Therefore take up the whole armor of God, that you may be able to withstand in the evil day, and having done all, to stand. Stand therefore, having girded your waist with truth, having put on the breastplate of righteousness, and having shod your feet with the preparation of the gospel of peace; above all, taking the shield of faith with which you will be able to quench all the fiery darts of the wicked one. And take the helmet of salvation, and the sword of the Spirit, which is the word of God; praying always with all prayer and supplication in the Spirit, being watchful to this end with all perseverance and supplication for all the saints—.'

Eph. 6:10-18 nkjv

'Do not be overcome by evil, but overcome evil with good.'

Romans 12:21

FOREWORD BY KURT CADDY

This is a children's book about fighting. These kinds of books are rare because most people don't teach their kids about fighting. And that is a shame because every kid (and adult) needs to learn about effective fighting. But this isn't the kind of fighting reserved for bullies and thugs. This is a spiritual fight for truth. Paul instructs a young Timothy to "Fight the good fight of faith…". Believers young and old need to learn about this "good fight". We need to aware of the spiritual warfare that is taking place all around us. Our Enemy seeks to "steal, kill and destroy." We must know who our Enemy is and how he works against us. In my experience, the Enemy likes to play the mind game. He toys with our thoughts long before he tempts us to act against God. What we think leads to what we do. So our archenemy uses such weapons as fear and doubt to bring about his purposes.

But our Deliverer, Jesus Christ, has already fought and secured our victory at the cross and through the resurrection! We are indeed "more than Conquerors". Our children need to be equipped to fight the spiritual battles that will come their way. It is not a matter of "if" they come, but "when" they come. Will they be ready and able to defend the truth in the face of doubt? Will they simply trust when fear rears its ugly head? These are important issues for our kids and it is never too early to train them for battle.

This book, written by a young believer, is a helpful tool to be used to train and equip other believers young and old. Read it often. Use it as a reference manual for future encounters with the Enemy. Let this book remind you and your children that we are conquerors and overcomers! And may these be days of victory! To God be the Glory!

Kurt Caddy
Director of University Ministries
Southwest Baptist University

Acknowledgements

I would like to thank my parents for their gift of time, wisdom, and ideas to help me in making this a reality. You were the motivation for this work when I did not want to continue, and I thank you for all you have done for me in bringing me to this moment.

Much thanks to Bo, my brother, for his ingenious ideas which helped with the development and naming of both some of the dragons and weapons. You are the brains where my own fail.

I would also like to thank Olivia Caddy. You are my chief publicist and my best friend. Thanks for everything.

I also send a hearty thank you to my brothers and all the children of my community, you give me inspiration and encouragement and constantly surprise me with your ideas and insights. Your delight over my hard work is loved. I strive to see you all smile.

FEAR

Believing you are not safe

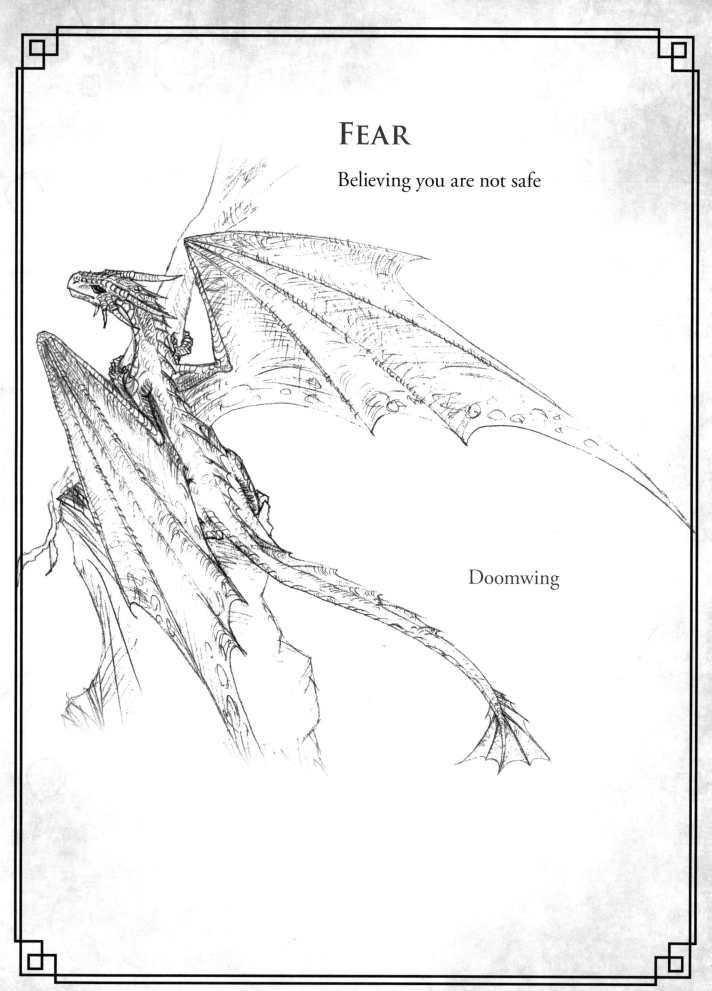

Doomwing

COURAGE

Standing up for right and putting your confidence in the Lord

'Have I not commanded you? Be strong and of good courage, do not be afraid nor be dismayed, for the Lord your God is with you wherever you go.' Joshua 1:9 nkjv

Shadowscarer

The Dragon:

Cowering in the depths of a cave, craggy cliff, old mountaintop monastery, castle, or any other disrepaired thing upon the heights in which a shadow may lurk, the fear dragon makes its abode. Dark as polished obsidian, with eyes like burning embers, the fear dragon waits. It's wings are big and angled sharply to help it with a swift and silent flight. Any dragon never stops growing, always getting too big for its intended prey to fight back. Armed with a deadly, almost invisible gas, the fear dragon breathes it over its enemies, which paralyzes them with fright once breathed in. When angered, the fear dragon emits a roar of sound so loud it has been likened to a thunderclap. The sound is very often accompanied by a bolt of yellowish lightening. A fearsome foe, the dragon is a match for anyone and everyone. Yet three things frighten a fear dragon. The first one is silver. All dragons fear silver, because it is poison to them and reflects the light, while to us, in small amounts is health. Second, the dragon fears courage. Third, the dragon fears the light, either spiritual or physical.

--I modeled the fear dragon to be swift, silent, big, and dark. Because isn't that what fear is? One minute you are perfectly fine, then you hear one noise, or notice the silence, or see something, and suddenly it is as if you have come face-to-face with a terrifying dragon. However, a light in darkness, a weapon of defense, or a companion can chase your fear (or dragon) away. The wonderful thing about God is that He is a friend, He is the Word, and the Word is a light to your path and a fearsome sword. No fear can overtake you when your confidence is in the Lord. 'For if God is for me, who can be against me?'

The Weapon:

The Shadowscarer (Shadow-scare-er), or the sword of courage, is a formidable weapon. The blade, made of polished steel, glows white in the dark and orange when evil nears. The bottom of the pommel is embedded with a large blue crystal that glows in the dark, too. The handle also has a gas reservoir with places for the gas to seep out on each guard prong. A button on the upper handle near the blade, when pressed, emits the gas into the air. Upon contact with the air, the gas bursts into flame, thereby giving you a double torch on either side of the blade. With a weapon for defense and a light in the dark, no Doomwing fear dragon would dare come near. The Lord has made you to be a shadowscarer…be one.

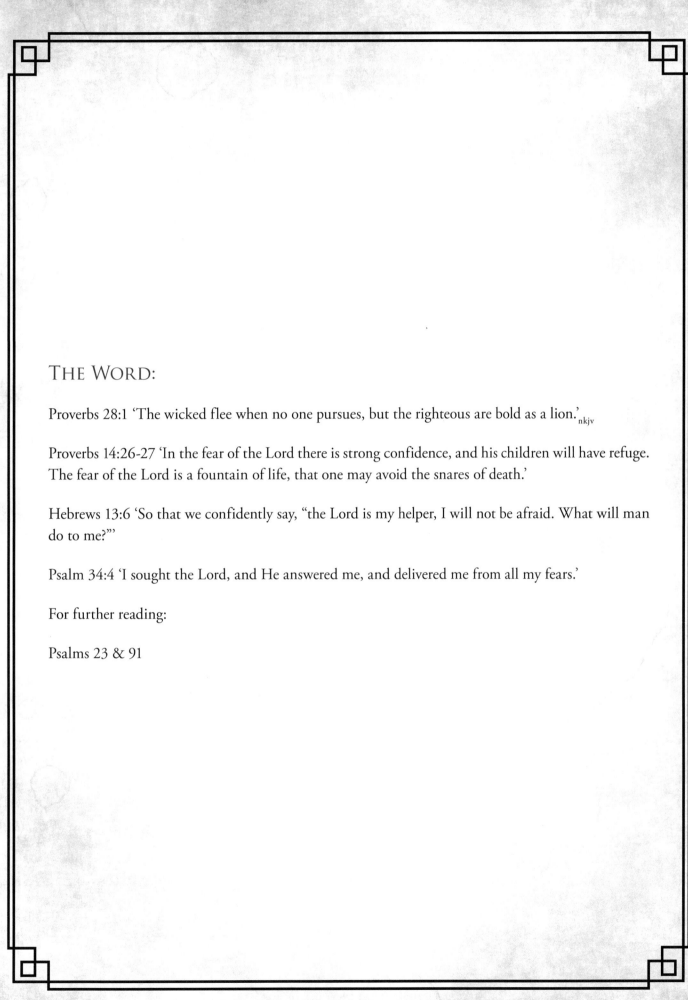

THE WORD:

Proverbs 28:1 'The wicked flee when no one pursues, but the righteous are bold as a lion.'nkjv

Proverbs 14:26-27 'In the fear of the Lord there is strong confidence, and his children will have refuge. The fear of the Lord is a fountain of life, that one may avoid the snares of death.'

Hebrews 13:6 'So that we confidently say, "the Lord is my helper, I will not be afraid. What will man do to me?"'

Psalm 34:4 'I sought the Lord, and He answered me, and delivered me from all my fears.'

For further reading:

Psalms 23 & 91

Selfishness

Putting yourself before others

Sandfire Shelfysh Dragons

SACRIFICE

Giving up something for the sake of someone else

'Greater love has no one than this, that
one lay down his life for his friends.'
John 15:13

R.R. (Reptile-Rifle)

THE DRAGON:

The dragons of selfishness live alone in burrows they dig out of the sand, rocks, and clay with their large, webbed front feet. These dragons are fiercely territorial, and always have a hoard, though what they hoard varies greatly. The only time they gather with other dragons is to raid villages and towns. Teaming up with many other types of sin-dragons, they descend upon the unsuspecting town, burning, destroying, and stealing the inhabitants' possessions and livelihood. Going into selfishness dragon territory is dangerous, but confronting the creature itself is even more perilous. Sandfire Shelfysh dragons breathe a cloud of sulphur dust, which is severely irritating to the eyes and skin. Many a traveler has become prey of the selfishness dragon; though, there is one peculiar thing about these beasts. They often imprison their prey in their lair, instead of immediately destroying it; so in defeating the dragon you will also be freeing the captured.

--Selfishness is the root of many a sin, because it is the act of putting ourselves first. Joy and fulfillment comes from putting God first, others second, and yourself last; but it is so easy to forget that. I created the selfishness dragons in a quarrel and they both have a good few spikes, because selfishness causes strife, and strife causes hurt. Sacrifice, on the other hand, is the total opposite of the selfish heart. Remember, the greatest kind of love is laying your life down for those you care about. That is true sacrifice, but it doesn't have to mean you have to die for someone. It means putting their needs before your own, with no intention of your own gain.

THE WEAPON:

In times past, fathers of the pioneers would always have a musket or rifle hung above their front door, to be used in emergency to protect their families. But a gun like this R.R. (that's reptile-rifle) is old-style; which means it takes at least twenty seconds to load. So, you're standing between an angry Sandfire dragon and the family you love, and you've got one shot and yourself to give, or your fear to give in to. Ready?

The Word:

Philippians 2:3-4 'Do nothing out of selfish ambition or vain conceit. Rather, in humility value others above yourselves, not looking to your own interests but each of you to the interests of the others.' niv

1 John 3:17 'But whoever has the world's goods, and sees his brother in need and closes his heart against him, how does the love of God abide in him?'

Romans 15:1-3 'We then that are strong ought to bear the infirmities of the weak, and not to please ourselves. Let every one of us please his neighbor for his good to edification. For even Christ pleased not himself...' kjv

For further reading:

Acts 20:35

BITTERNESS

Being unwilling to forgive someone

Kaawi Kambwe Dragon

Forgiveness

Being willing to completely release a wrong done to you

'Bearing with one another, and forgiving each other, whoever has a complaint against anyone; just as the Lord forgave you, so also should you.' Colossians 3:13

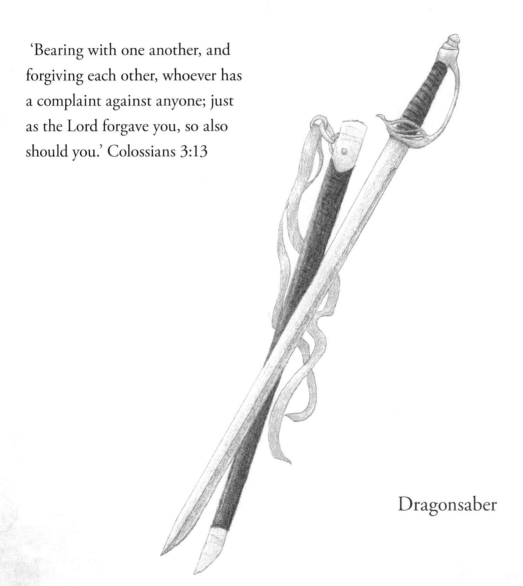

Dragonsaber

THE DRAGON:

Standing atop a windblown slope, its wings battered from wind and cold, the bitterness dragon stands. Its small, fiery, dark eyes glare, looking for something. It never forgets or forgives a trespasser, even though its territory spans up to two-hundred miles. Not far away, you stand in the snow, alone because you quarreled with your comrades and left them behind. They'd been rubbing you raw for a while now, and finally you've decided to leave them. You don't really need or want them anymore. As you walk, the frozen wind claws at your skin, and the white dragony shape that looks like a rock is watching you. It's been watching you for a long time, waiting for you to be alone and vulnerable. The white shape takes flight, it's ragged wings looking as if they blend directly into the sky. It takes your breath away, but if it has any beauty it is short-lived. The creature roars into the atmosphere, lands about one-hundred fifty feet away, and stalks toward you. Roaring again, the beast growls, its sinister form emanating hostility. Your comrades flash through your mind. If your bitterness hadn't caused you to leave them and tromp out alone, you wouldn't be in this mess. Should you run?

--I named the bitterness dragon the Kaawi Kambwe. These are two Lugandan words, the first of which means bitter, icy, and cold; and the second meaning terror, angry, and fierce. This is exactly what bitterness is. It is purely unforgiveness, or holding a grudge, as some call it. Bitterness is a dangerous thing. Why? Because it is the maker of villains. It is the father of wars. It is the wedge that holds apart healing. Forgiveness, on the other hand, is imbedded in God's message to us. It is the core of how he made us new creatures. He says as you forgive others, so he will forgive you. He wants to forgive us, and for us to forgive, yet we vow "to never speak to that person again" and other such things. The scenario above comes from harboring bitterness in our heart. Eventually it will grow until it explodes, like the gas breath the dragon breathes, made of hydrogen that it lights with its tail. Bitterness stems from unforgiveness and is a powerful vice. Forgiveness stems from love and is even more powerful. We need Him to break the impulse of anger and hate, and help us choose to forgive. Only God can help you break that vice and give you the joy of being a conqueror, bearing love as a banner, and grace as a sword. (Note: the word trespass has two meanings in the text: intrude and sin.)

THE WEAPON:

The Dragonsaber is a sword of legend. Long ago, the same sword was responsible for a wound to the dragon's right foreleg. Being bitter, the dragon never let it heal. It hopes you will never return with such a thing as that sword of forgiveness again; but if you do, it will try its best to make you get rid of it. You will only be the dragon's prey if you let your weapon go. So, will you be ruthless with the Kaawi Kambwe and forgive others? Or will you spare the dragon and hurt much more?

THE WORD:

Ephesians 4:31 'Let all bitterness and wrath and anger and clamor and slander be put away from you, along with all malice.'

Proverbs 24:17 'Do not rejoice when your enemy falls, and do not let your heart be glad when he stumbles.'

Luke 6:27-29 'But I say to you who hear, love your enemies, do good to those who hate you, bless those who curse you, pray for those who mistreat you. Whoever hits you on the cheek, offer him the other also; and whoever takes away your coat, do not withhold your shirt from him either.'

Philippians 4:8 'Finally brothers, whatever is true, whatever is noble, whatever is right, whatever is pure, whatever is lovely, whatever is admirable—if anything is excellent or praiseworthy—think on such things.' niv

For further reading:

Romans 12: 14, 19-20

Laziness

Being slack in your actions, not accomplishing your work to the best of your ability

Acidic Lazidorre

DILIGENCE

Doing the best we can do in the tasks given to us

Whatever your hand finds to
do, do it with all your might.'
Ecclesiastes 9:10$_{niv}$

Dragonslayer

The Dragon:

Known to move with turtle-like slowness and specialize in looking always half-asleep, the Acidic Lazidorre or laziness dragon is purely lazy. It never moves farther than three hundred yards from its lair (except in the event of being extremely frightened, in which a dragon of this type made it three miles once). Even its wings hang limp, seeming to have shrunk with disuse. It would be the fattest dragon alive had it not made out to survive on so little. This beast, on the outside, seems to care for nothing and no one. But though the laziness dragon appears incredibly slow, it is really like a heron or hawk, patiently waiting for prey to appear. Anything that ventures close enough under the false impression that this beast is no match for them will soon find a creature they are no match for. Once their intended quarry has gotten close enough, Laziness dragons move with the speed of an angered crocodile. Since this dragon appears harmless but is deadly, laziness dragons are often found guarding castles, prisoners, or treasure; sitting like toll keepers on bridges or lonely roads, luring in the unsuspecting. They also possess the ability to breathe acid, which they do not hesitate to wield against those that anger them, or those they wish to stop that they deem too far away. One must match the unpredictability and ferocity of such a dragon if they wish to win and survive.

--Laziness can sometimes sneak up before we know it, coming out in complaining and whiny words before we expect. The dragon's tactics are similar. Once you see the dragon pounce or spit acid you immediately know the beast's power, although before, you hardly knew what to expect. Laziness is dangerous, as God warns the one who is lazy is brother to him who destroys. In the case of this dragon that statement can be quite literal. By contrast, diligence is a prized possession. Which one will you choose? Destruction or treasure?

The Weapon:

This sword is known by the name of the Dragonslayer, and its design manifests its name. Beautiful, well-made, and strong, this tool's blade appears to be sharpened to an almost translucent edge. The blue crystal dragon wound about the handle, the ruby fire encrusted into the steel, reflect the quality of the weapon. Its maker truly made it with all his might. Now go and use it with all yours plus the authority the Lord has given you to vanquish any lazy Lazidorres that come your way.

The Word:

Proverbs 22:29 'Seest thou a man diligent in his business? He will stand before kings; he will not stand before mean men.'_{kjv}

Galatians 6:9 'Let us not become weary in doing good, for at the proper time we will reap a harvest if we do not give up.'_{niv}

Proverbs 14:23 'In all labor there is profit, but mere talk leads only to poverty.'

Proverbs 18:9 'One who is slack in his work is brother to one who destroys.'_{niv}

Colossians 3:23 'Whatever you do, work at it with all your heart, as working for the Lord, not for human masters (men).'_{niv}

For further reading:

1 Corinthians 15:58, Proverbs 15:19

PRIDE

Thinking of yourself as better than others

Gold Peacock Pridessence Dragon

HUMILITY

Knowing everything good in my life, including things
I have done, is a gift from God

'The reward of humility and the
fear of the Lord are riches, honor
and life.' Proverbs 22:4

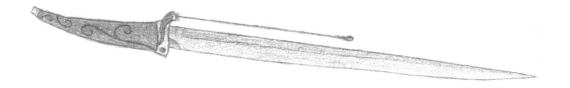

The Ancedere

THE DRAGON:

While walking in the forested lands of the great outdoors, you may come across a gold-scaled dragon staring into its reflection in a forest pool, licking its scales to a shine, or standing with its wings spread, its eyes half shut, sunning itself. You will know at first sight it is a pride dragon, with the full name of Gold Peacock Pridessence Dragon. Gold scaled, often seen strutting like a peacock, and embodying the essence of pride, this dragon is amply named. Dragons are very difficult to sneak up on, and even though the dragon may not have moved, it may know very well that you are there. Once the pride dragon has pounced, it can bite, scratch, and utilize its breath weapon of boiling water and high pitched sound to your terror and discomfort. If the dragon is bigger, it will make a show of stalking you down, flexing its muscles, and snarling (the bigger ones do not use the high pitched sound). The only thing that will save you from being beaten, burned, or eaten, is keeping a quick and discerning eye, a level head, and a humble heart. Gloat and you'll be in trouble; but know that everything you accomplish is a gift given by God, and you'll come out the victor.

--Pride loves to show itself off. I made the Pride dragon gold-scaled with purple-blue circles on his wings and similar accents on his feet and head so it had something to be prideful about. Pride comes from putting ourselves above others, thinking for whatever reason we are better than they. It is when we stop recognizing everything is a gift from God, when we start to think everything we have is brought about by our own strength. It says in the Word, God opposes the proud. To oppose is to basically fight against. God, the King and most powerful being of the universe, is definitely *not* the one you want to be fighting against, for He is your power and you are nothing without Him.

THE WEAPON:

Humility's weapon, the Ancedere, isn't much to look at. But it is much more than it seems. The handle, curved slightly, is a horn to blow for emergencies or warnings. It is also equipped with a secret reservoir for acid, which can be shot out of one of the guard handles using a trigger button. Oh, and did I mention the blade is actually diamond, which means it can cut through practically anything? And the blade glows in the dark. Pretty awesome, and yet, be careful! Boast about your own strength, and the blade will bend, the light fade, the acid dwindle…you can imagine the consequence. To avoid this, remember that what you have, including your weapon and your life, is from God. So boast in the God you have, He is your strength! Do this…and those Pridessence dragons better watch out.

The Word:

Proverbs 3:5-6 'Trust in the Lord with all of your heart and lean not on your own understanding. In all your ways acknowledge Him, and He will direct your paths. Do not be wise in your own eyes; fear the Lord and turn away from evil.' _{nkjv}

Proverbs 16:18 'Pride goes before destruction, and a haughty spirit before a fall.' _{nkjv}

Proverbs 27:1-2 'Do not boast about tomorrow, for you do not know what a day may bring forth. Let another man praise you, and not your own mouth; a stranger, and not your own lips.' _{nkjv}

Proverbs 28:25 'An arrogant man stirs up strife, but he who trusts in the Lord will prosper.'

Romans 12:16 'Be of the same mind toward one another; do not be haughty in mind, but associate with the lowly. Do not be wise in your own estimation.'

For further reading:

1 Peter 5:5-6

Idolatry

Excessive devotion or reverence to something other than God

Falsegold Edelatry Dragon

Fear of the Lord

Recognizing how powerful God is compared to us and in response we desire to trust and obey Him

Scaleblaster

'And you shall love the Lord your God with all your heart, with all your soul, with all your mind, and with all your strength.'
Mark 12:30_{nkjv}

The Dragon:

The Falsegold Edelatry dragon is dangerous, because it is a creature of sneaking deceit. The top portion of its horns, wings, back, and tail are all gold colored. But beneath on the creature's underbelly, the underside of his wings, sides, face, and legs are all a dismal grey that worsens in color with age. Since the top bit of it is gold and its wings are large, the Edelatry dragon will try to hide in the stippled sunlight of the forests and fields, like a tiger does, searching for prey. Any avid nature enthusiast that climbs the hills or sits near the rivers with the intent of watching, drawing, approaching, or taming any beauty of God's creation is in danger of the idolatry dragon. Hard to see because of the gold and grey, the dragon has the advantage until it gets within one hundred feet. Then the dragon is much easier to recognize in comparison with the plants, trees, and creatures of nature. But then you must be prepared, for often idolatry is so close you don't see it until it is too late. You must keep your weapon close and recognize the beast before it strikes.

--Recognizing real idolatry from harmless interest before it is too late is often as hard as telling the dragon from the forest in the illustration above. Things we admire, like, enjoy, or do can easily push into a danger zone. We must ask ourselves three questions: One, am I glorifying God with what I am doing? Two, is what I am doing taking away from, or more important to me than being, talking with, and worshiping God? And three, is this action or interest wise?

The Weapon:

The fear of the Lord is manifested in this weapon, the Scaleblaster, because it isn't exactly big and awesome, nor is it equipped with rapid-fire. No, you've got your old-fashioned one-shot pistol complete with silver bullets, which you remember is poison to dragons. The defining feature of this little handgun is only your fear of the King of kings, because He is your sword, your power, your protector. You know the idolatry dragon will get as close to you as possible before striking, and even though shooting a dragon at point-blank range seems like a smart idea, NEVER let the creature get that close. If you see a Falsegold Edelatry dragon approach you, pray for victory…and fire! And…fire! And be ready to reload, idolatry is prone to attack more than once.

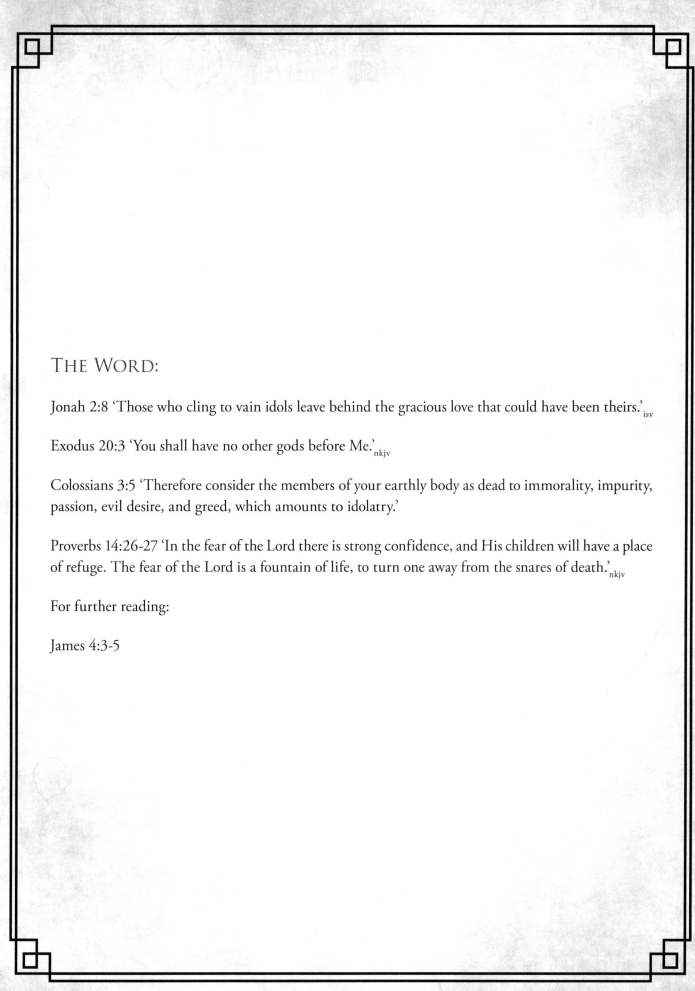

THE WORD:

Jonah 2:8 'Those who cling to vain idols leave behind the gracious love that could have been theirs.'_{isv}

Exodus 20:3 'You shall have no other gods before Me.'_{nkjv}

Colossians 3:5 'Therefore consider the members of your earthly body as dead to immorality, impurity, passion, evil desire, and greed, which amounts to idolatry.'

Proverbs 14:26-27 'In the fear of the Lord there is strong confidence, and His children will have a place of refuge. The fear of the Lord is a fountain of life, to turn one away from the snares of death.'_{nkjv}

For further reading:

James 4:3-5

DECEITFULNESS

Hiding or distorting the truth

Nataserpent

Truthfulness

Being honest no matter what

'…the truth shall make you free.'
John 8:32b~nkjv~

The Conquerer

The Dragon:

Slipping amongst the foliage and dappled sunlight of any forest or jungle, perhaps coiling its slender, winged body about the branches of a tree, the serpentine dragon of deceit keeps its eyes alert, its teeth bared. Like the serpent from whence it came, these creatures often live in fruit trees, poisoning the air about by its ability to speak in a hissy, lilting voice. They breathe gas and spitballs of fire, and love to exert their abilities upon humans of any kind. You must not listen to this dragon, nor stay near it. The gas this beast breathes, as well as the lies in its mouth, can quickly shut off your mind to its danger. Use your sword and the authority God's given you, for a lie is only powerful when it's believed.

--You can easily see I created this dragon to resemble the serpent in the garden of Eden. Deceitfulness, lying, or not telling the whole truth are dangers that are easy to fall prey to. All of us have thought at some point that telling only part of the truth or twisting it altogether is better than getting the consequence we deserve. But when you give into lies once, you better beware, because the lies will increase both in size and quantity. The Lord cautions us also against believing lies, and they are in abundance, for 'the world is in the sway of the wicked one.' Bring everything back to the Word, and do not sell His truth for a lie! The truth, and only the truth (for God is the truth) can set you free.

The Weapon:

A broad-sword at its best, Truth is the classic sword of courage used by heroes, knights, and dragon-slayers for millennia. Its formal name is the Conquerer. Its age-old brilliance will always be remembered by the ever-enslaving, evil-spreading sin-dragons, including the old foe, Nataserpent (a.k.a. Deceit). Truth's blade can separate truth from lie, good from evil, and the Nataserpent is deathly afraid of it. But, as a master of deceit, he may not show it. Wield it for the freedom it lives for, so that sin may no longer hold you in bondage.

THE WORD:

James 3:5 'Likewise, the tongue is a small part of the body, but it makes great boasts. Consider what a great forest is set on fire by a small spark.'_{niv}

Psalm 34:12-14 'Who is the man who desires life, and loves many days, that he may see good? Keep your tongue from evil and your lips from speaking deceit. Depart from evil and do good; seek peace and pursue it.'_{nkjv}

Psalm 37:30 'The mouth of the righteous speaks wisdom, and his tongue talks of justice.'_{nkjv}

Proverbs 12: 18-20 'There is one who speaks rashly like the thrusts of a sword, but the tongue of the wise brings healing. Truthful lips will be established forever, but a lying tongue is only for a moment. Deceit is in the heart of those who devise evil, but counselors of peace have joy.'

Proverbs 14:25 'A truthful witness saves lives, but the person who lies is deceitful.'_{isv}

Psalm 25:3 'Indeed, let no one who waits on You be ashamed; Let those be ashamed who deal treacherously without cause.'_{nkjv}

For further reading:

John 8:31-36 and James 3

DISOBEDIENCE

Neglecting or not doing what I am supposed to do

Thunderrex

OBEDIENCE

Doing what is expected of me right away, with a happy heart, and doing a good job

'Children, obey your parents in all things, for this is well pleasing to the Lord.' Colossians 3:20 nkjv

Fireblade

THE DRAGON:

Creeping along a cavern wall, footsteps echoing, you find yourself peering around for any sign of scales or claws. You're here to find the dragon that has been terrorizing your home and family—the Thunderrex. Nothing. Relaxing slightly, you slink forward until stepping to the edge of a huge cavern room. At the far edge, you see an orange light, probably from lava flow. Stepping out into the open takes courage, but finally you attempt it…only to hear wicked growls sounding somewhat like laughter seep into your ears. The sound grows louder, and out of the shadows rises a huge greenish dragon with maroon and black around the edges. Snickering and snarling, the dragon's eyes light with what appears to be triumph, but you see fear beneath that mask. Readying your fire-sword, you wait, glaring back at the fiendish creature. He stops snarling and roars, flapping his wings, and then stomps forward. You light your sword. The fight is on.

--Disobedience is fierce or subtle, though because it is one of the major sins that people fight I wanted the dragon to be big. If obedience is obeying right away, with a happy heart, and doing a good job; than forgetting any one of those points is disobedience. If you obey while complaining, it's not obedience, because obedience is with a happy heart. I know it's hard, but obedience has its rewards. You become more trustworthy, more joyful, and obedience becomes easier, because hearing the Lord's voice clearer than before, you will be able to know and trust what God wants for you. Choose to obey, and see what blessing God bestows on an obedient heart.

THE WEAPON:

A Fireblade is a fire-sword! A long pole covered with flammable fluid that can be replenished with a push of a button, or ignited with another button, graces the back of a long silver samurai-like blade. Swing this at any dragon and watch his eyes widen at your weapon's rivalry. But…you're working with fire and flammable items and sharp steel, which means, the careless are those that get hurt. Never touch the blade or pole anywhere! Disobey that, and your hand will be in trouble. Oh, and a tip about Thunderrex Disobedience dragons: they're aggravated by fire; and even though they breathe it, the scales on their backs between their wings are not fireproof. Be obedient, and show the power of your sword!

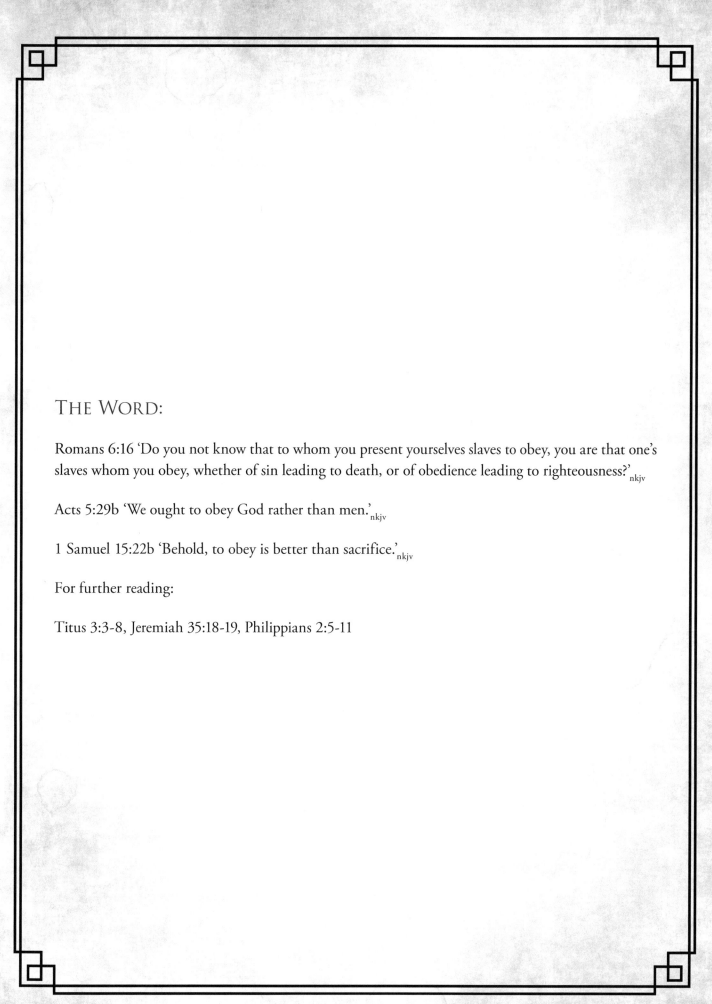

THE WORD:

Romans 6:16 'Do you not know that to whom you present yourselves slaves to obey, you are that one's slaves whom you obey, whether of sin leading to death, or of obedience leading to righteousness?' [nkjv]

Acts 5:29b 'We ought to obey God rather than men.' [nkjv]

1 Samuel 15:22b 'Behold, to obey is better than sacrifice.' [nkjv]

For further reading:

Titus 3:3-8, Jeremiah 35:18-19, Philippians 2:5-11

WORRY

Having fear about what could happen

Blugadrac Wirrye Dragon

TRUST

Believing that God's will is always right and good

'Casting all your anxiety on Him, because He cares for you.' 1 Peter 5:7

Bowsirspear

35

THE DRAGON:

The Blugadrac Wirrye dragon is constantly looking over his shoulder, hesitating before doing anything, and sometimes not doing anything at all, for fear of something going wrong. Though it has large wings capable of marvelous flying, it fears crashing and often postpones landing or doesn't leave the ground. It always thinks something is lurking behind a tree, and because of this the worry dragon is very hard to get near to. And, if the dragon allows you to get close and begins bickering to you about this and that danger and constant "what if's," or while walking you hear anxious whispers nearby, get out of there and fast! The worry dragon is trying to lure you into its worrying trap with its words and its poisonous thought gas. Once it has you worried sick, it becomes a fierce and deceptive predator, ready to pounce, instead of a worried winged lizard. Beware! If it is not worried itself, it will worry your mind until your fears come true in the form of the Wirrye dragon making you its prey.

--Worry. We often do it, and can't really help it, it seems. Yet Jesus said not to worry about anything. By worrying, we aren't trusting God to take care of us. Doesn't he care enough to know us all personally? Didn't He care enough to take your sins upon Himself? Doesn't He pay enough attention to know when a sparrow dies? Then surely, He knows about you and all your worries and fears and needs. He will take care of you. He knows; trust Him.

THE WEAPON:

This multi-weapon, the Bowsirspear, is both surprising and useful. A long-spear or dragon-spear that doubles as an axe, the spearhead can be slid off and used as a sword. Also, the spear shaft can twist and snap into a bow for shooting arrows. When finished with your sword and bow, you can snap them back together as a dragon-spear again. A strong weapon, like God's Word, you can definitely trust in this tool to pose a serious threat to any Blugadrac Wirrye dragons that dare to come near. Go prepared and win!

The Word:

Philippians 4:6-7 'Be anxious for nothing, but in everything by prayer and supplication, with thanksgiving, let your requests be made known to God; and the peace of God, which surpasses all understanding, will guard your hearts and minds through Christ Jesus.' nkjv

Proverbs 12:25 'Anxiety in a man's heart weighs it down, but a good word makes it glad.'

Psalm 37:5 'Commit your way to the Lord, trust also in Him, and He will do it.'

For further reading:

Matthew 6: 25-34 or Luke 12:24-34

GREED

Never being content with what we have, always wanting more

Chandekalen Greade Dragon

GENEROSITY

Giving to others out of our love for Christ without expecting anything in return

'But seek first His kingdom and His righteousness, and all these things will be added to you.' Matthew 6:33

The Eagle-arrow

THE DRAGON:

The lair of a Chandekalen Greade dragon is located in the depths of the earth below a desert or canyon; and it is always heaped with treasure. The horde is gathered from kingdoms fallen, villages burned, ships sunk, and other dragons' lairs. Never having enough, the greed dragon will always be out on another expedition, gathering gold and spreading destruction. It will even fight and kill others of its kind to get at their treasure stores. At home, you'll find him lying atop his treasure, sometimes half-burying himself in the gold, sleeping or sorting his treasure, his eyes mirroring the glinting metal at his feet. This beast is a wyvern, or a dragon with only two feet. With plated grey-black scales and fire breath, the greed Dragon is a fearsome foe. Often the lair has a pool of melted gold in it, made of the trinkets the dragon has melted because they were not fine enough to look at. This pool, once hardened, is a mirror for the ugly beast to stare at its reflection.

--Be on your guard venturing into this dragon's lair. The sight of tons of gold, seemingly sitting there for the taking, could make any person's heart greedy. But the greed dragon lingers in the shadows, and with it, its gas breath capable of turning your mind to the love of money. Beware of thinking as the dragon would, "I never have enough, I'll never let a single person share it with me, I'm willing to do anything to keep it safe or get more for myself." Once you begin to think like this, wanting to keep it all and have more, you'll want to keep the greed (dragon) alive, too. But to the dragon, you're not its master, you're its prey.

THE WEAPON:

The winged Eagle-arrows crafted to combat Chandekalen Greade Dragons are a thing of beauty. Built with a double set of miniature "wings" on the tail end of each arrow, this construction allows the arrow to slightly adjust its flight path, avoiding good and striking evil. They are sharp enough to pierce the toughest dragon hide, and yet they will not puncture any servant of God. These arrows are precious, and use them well; yet, give some away to those in need. Who knows, maybe one of those arrows might save *your* life someday.

THE WORD:

Proverbs 15:16 'Better is a little with the fear of the Lord than great treasure and turmoil with it.'

Luke 6:34 'If you lend to those from whom you expect to receive, what credit is that to you? Even sinners lend to sinners in order to receive back the same amount.'

1 Timothy 6: 9-10 'But those who want to get rich fall into temptation and a snare and many foolish and harmful desires which plunge men into ruin and destruction. For the love of money is a root of all sorts of evil, and some by longing for it have wandered away from the faith and pierced themselves with many griefs.'

Hebrews 13:5 'Make sure that your character is free from the love of money, being content with what you have; for He Himself has said, "I will never desert you, nor will I ever forsake you."'

For further reading:

Matthew 6:19-21

DISHONOR

Treating others with disrespect

Zurinor

HONOR

Viewing others through God's eyes and treating them as better then ourselves

'Honor all people, love the brotherhood, fear God, honor the king.' 1 Peter 2:17

Serpentlance

The Dragon:

Dishonor dragons (Zurinors) have three to seven heads, and all of the heads will never pay attention to the same thing at once. Terrible in its manners, it lives in the bogs and marshes, smelling horrible and catching and eating fish, young alligators, and whatever and whoever else comes into its territory. If you ever come across it, it will never honor you with its full attention, though it will commit enough of it to corner you into its trap. You may notice the dragon's frills. These two large webby appendages are used to glide through the air, and the dragon makes good use of this advantage, as well as its stinky, misty cloud of acidic breath. Also, they hunt in packs, and are hefty with insults and abusive words. As always, be careful and arm yourself!

--Lack of honor can be the source of many kinds of strife, misunderstanding, and grudges. Stemming from selfishness or pride, dishonor itself threatens us with its abundance. We could still obey our parents…but give them a hateful backwards glance just to show our distaste for such a task; however, that is dishonor and not real obedience. Honor is necessary. Faith demands honor, and honor needs faith. One of the primary things that distinguish great men and women is their honor for God and for others. Choose to honor those around you, and see how God works.

The Weapon:

Honor's Serpentlance is your good old dragon-spear. Eight feet long, with a silver head three feet in length, this weapon will rival any dragon's biggest spikes. Tie your colors below the point and hold it proud, it was meant to be used with honor! (Which means you don't wallop someone over the head with it.) Like the lances of the Middle Ages, this tool is often used in what they call pitched battle (which means they organize everyone and everything really nicely before charging like mad at each other). Wave this piece of sheer craftsmanship in any of Zurinor's faces and he won't stick around long enough for you to organize an honorary pitched battle with him…after all, he's a dishonor dragon.

The Word:

Ephesians 6:1-3 'Children, obey your parents in the Lord, for this is right. "Honor your father and mother"—which is the first commandment with a promise— "so that it may go well with you and that you may enjoy long life on the earth."'niv

2 Timothy 2:20-21 'But in a great house there are not only vessels of gold and silver, but also of wood and clay, some for honor and some for dishonor. Therefore if anyone cleanses himself from the latter (dishonor), he will be a vessel for honor, sanctified and useful for the Master, prepared for every good work.'nkjv

Hebrews 5:4 'And no one takes the honor to himself, but receives it when he is called by God, even as Aaron was.'

Romans 12:10 'Be devoted to one another in love. Honor one another above yourselves.'niv

For further reading:

Romans 12:1-2 & 9-13, Matthew 22:36-40

INDISCIPLINE

Lacking obedience to the Holy Spirit and control of ourselves

Dikklewings

SELF-CONTROL

Giving up our own desires to the Holy Spirit's control

'Be alert and of sober mind (self-controlled, sound-minded). Your enemy the devil prowls around like a roaring lion looking for someone to devour. Resist him, standing firm in the faith.' 1 Peter 5:8-9a niv

Staffblade

The Dragon:

Indiscipline dragons live in old ruins or misty mountain cliffs or bays where the fog is so thick you often can't see twenty feet ahead of you. Living in packs or clans, the indiscipline dragons will gang up on prey, viciously chasing them until they succeed in bringing it down. These dragons breathe plasma bolts: fireballs mingled with lightening that explode upon contact. Their brown bodies are streaked with orange, yellow, and blue. Sharp spines protrude from their necks down to the tip of their tails, and a double-pronged crest grows as the dragon ages, getting up to one-third as big as the dragon's head. Lastly, when the dragon exceeds twenty years, the spines on its tail and neck begin to grow faster and loosen, which the dragon will sling like throwing knives. Fighting the relentlessness and ferocity of these spiny dragons can be tough. They are unpredictable, fierce, and ravenous in pursuit of their prey. The only way to succeed is to be self-controlled and trust God. Lose your head, and you just might end up slammed into a rock face.

--Indiscipline is lack of self-control. Indiscipline dragons were supposed to be that way, uncouth in their eating, harmful in their build, and undisciplined in their actions. They follow feeling, want, and the wish of whimsy. Living in packs or wandering alone, these creatures do what they want, many times to their downfall (note: only about 1 out of every 3 of these beasts lives to 20 years old). This dragon often comes from our sinful flesh and not who we are in Christ. Indiscipline is such a dangerous thing. The Lord admonished us in Paul's letter to Timothy 'be self-controlled in all things.' If we can't put to use our God-given authority to resist temptation, it can only be to our harm.

The Weapon:

Called the Staffblade, this weapon takes skill to handle. Three handles for maneuverability, two blades and two points for defense; yet if you slide your hands off the handles you risk cutting them on the sharp steel. As the Bible says, 'be self-controlled and alert' when handling this tool. This weapon is as tall as a staff, and can be swung, thrust, thrown, or spun, giving you the ability to use it like a sword, spear, ax, or quarterstaff. It is a remarkable sword against Dikklewings, the dragons of Indiscipline. Handle it well!

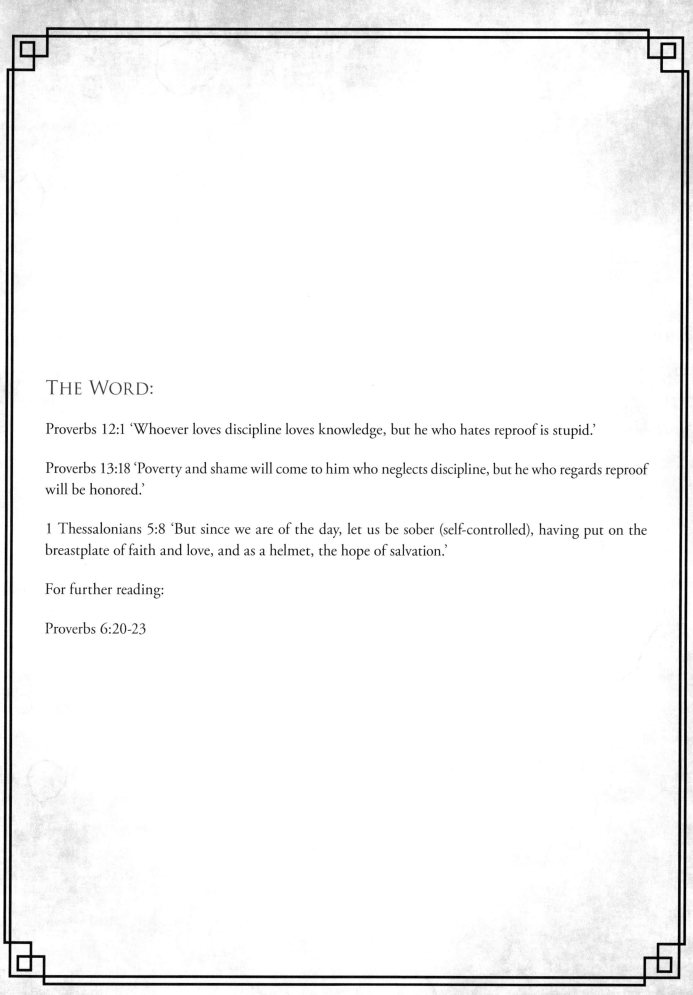

The Word:

Proverbs 12:1 'Whoever loves discipline loves knowledge, but he who hates reproof is stupid.'

Proverbs 13:18 'Poverty and shame will come to him who neglects discipline, but he who regards reproof will be honored.'

1 Thessalonians 5:8 'But since we are of the day, let us be sober (self-controlled), having put on the breastplate of faith and love, and as a helmet, the hope of salvation.'

For further reading:

Proverbs 6:20-23

Lavawing Inkinde Dragon

UNKINDNESS

Using our actions and words to harm others

KINDNESS

Treating others as you would like to be treated,
knowing they are special creations of God

'What is desirable in a man is his kindness.'
Proverbs 19:22a

Lightsoar

The Dragon:

Standing in awe of a huge mountain seeping with lava, its backdrop on fire from the sunset, suddenly you think you see a silhouette, dragon-shaped, glide between mountain crags and clouds. But maybe it was your imagination. No, you see it once more, swooping low above the lava, sending a plume of flame to meet the molten stone. As it rises, it lifts its head, abruptly turns, and flies off. Did it see you? Maybe not. Turning away, you take one last look at the glowing mountain. Then, out of the clouds tinted with smoke and sunset, the dragon strikes. Ducking to avoid sharp talons and an explosion of fire, you look up to see the dragon again. Its red scales glinting and horns pointed forward, the dragon roars at the sky before turning in flight and diving at you again. Unable to escape, would anyone in his right mind not draw his sword?

The Unkindness dragon is a mysterious beast. This creature breathes fire and often destroys the castles or volcanic lairs it is found in, at the slightest hint of an unlikable situation. Why? Because this dragon often lives in fear or hate. Fear that its eggs will be stolen or its home destroyed, hate of other dragons and humans as well. The Unkindness dragon has been known to have up to thirty homes within its lifetime, and it always lives alone. Fighting an unkindness dragon takes skill. Remember to fight to the glory of God. Patience and precision are what will win a fight with this dragon.

--Unkindness is a demonstration of being fearful, listening to your flesh, or losing self-control. We are unkind in our words, actions, and thoughts toward other people. Fearing for ourselves and others, we aim our words and actions like weapons, to sting and inflict harm. In the book of James, God tells us that we should not use our tongues to both bless and curse. Elsewhere God also tells us to be self-controlled. Live in the Lord's confidence and trust, forgive and exercise self-control. Use the powerful tools of actions and words to honor the Lord, not inflict harm.

The Weapon:

A unique sword indeed, this weapon is specialized because it will not harm good. That's right, swing Kindness' Lightsoar at any good thing, your horse for example, and it will pass right through it! That's because the Lightsoar's blade is made of concentrated light; and of course, the dark hates the light. Lavawing Inkinde Dragons can breathe fire, and they love lava, but the pure light of the Lightsoar is cool and bright, and will slice through the heat, smoke, claws and scales of your fiery foes. Be merciless with evil, gentle with people, and shine your light, and the world will see your "kind" as never before!

THE WORD:

Luke 6:35 'But love your enemies, and do good, and lend, expecting nothing in return; and your reward will be great, and you will be sons of the Most High; for He Himself is kind to ungrateful and evil men.'

Ephesians 4:32 'And be kind to one another, tenderhearted, forgiving one another, even as God in Christ forgave you.'nkjv

Psalm 133:1 'Behold, how good and how pleasant it is for brothers to dwell together in unity!'

For further reading:

1 Peter 3:8-9

About the Author:

16 year old Grace M. M. Jaeger has been drawing and writing since she was little. Nothing delights her more than sharing truth that is exciting and inspiring through art and story. The eldest of seven children, Grace lives with her family near Springfield, Missouri.

Printed in the United States
By Bookmasters